Place a photo of you and your Pop Pop here

Text copyright © 2006 by Irene Smalls

Illustrations copyright © 2006 by Cathy Ann Johnson

Little, Brown and Company

Time Warner Book Group
1271 Avenue of the Americas, New York, NY 10020
Visit our Web site at www.lb-kids.com

First Edition: May 2006

Library of Congress Cataloging-in-Publication Data

Smalls, Irene.
  My Pop Pop and me / by Irene Smalls ; illustrated by Cathy Ann Johnson.— 1st ed.
    p. cm.
  Summary: A young boy who loves to sniff the lemon whiff and to clink the dishes
in the sink helps his Pop Pop bake a cake.
  ISBN 0-316-73422-5 (hardcover)
  [1. Baking—Fiction. 2. Cake—Fiction. 3. Stories in rhyme.] I. Johnson, Cathy Ann,
1964- ill. II. Title.
PZ8.3.S636Myap 2006
[ε]—dc22

                                                              2005022559

                    10 9 8 7 6 5 4 3 2 1

                            TWP

                     Printed in Singapore

                 Book design by Tracy Shaw

          The illustrations were done in water-based paints
                on Crescent Strathmore watercolor board.

             The text was set in Lebensjoy Medium,
              and the display type is Woodland ITC.

In memory of my dad, Clint: I can still smell
your peach cobbler baking in the oven.
A little something for your sweet tooth. —C.A.J.

Also by Irene Smalls:

My Nana and Me
Kevin and His Dad
Because You're Lucky
Jonathan and His Mommy
Irene and the Big, Fine Nickel

For my Great-Uncle Clarence Pierce, who said I was his favorite
and taught me "I love you Black Child." —I.S.

Clarence Pierce, Irene's Pop Pop

My Pop Pop and Me

by **Irene Smalls**

Illustrated by

Cathy Ann Johnson

LITTLE, BROWN AND COMPANY

New York · Boston

Look look   my Pop Pop's a cook

Pat pat   I love my chef's hat

SUGAR

Scrub a dub dub

clean and rub

Bake bake

my favorite cake

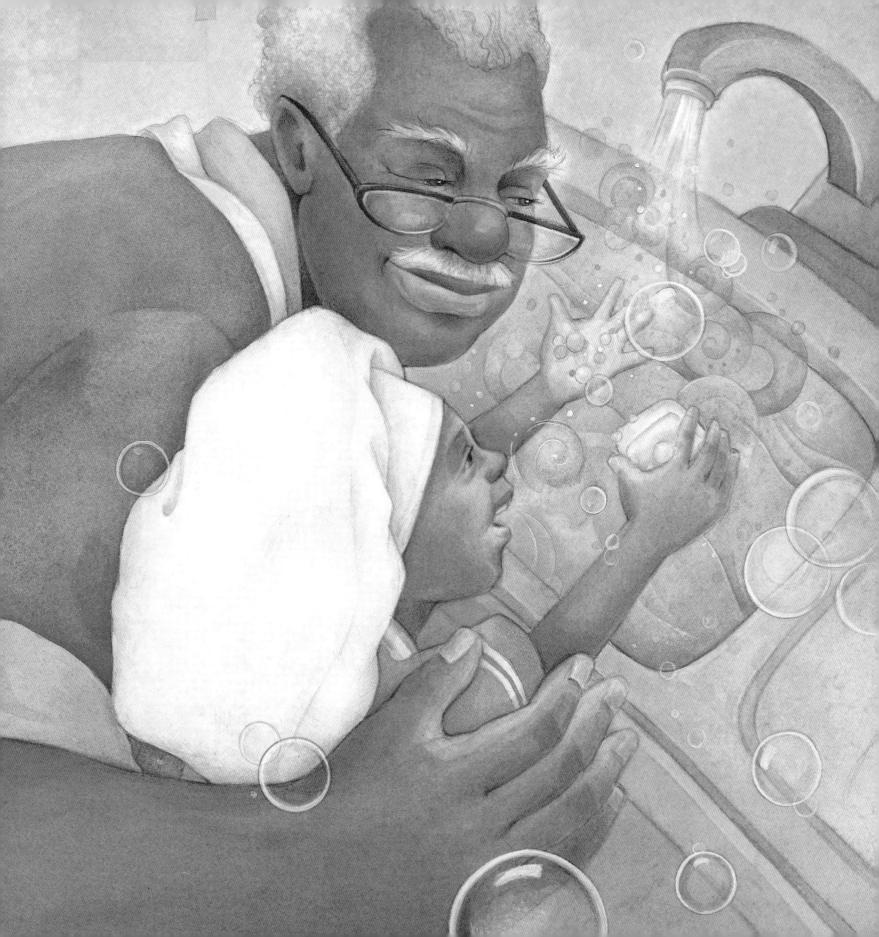

Sniff sniff the lemon whiff

Peel peel I love the lemon feel

Pish pish the lemon till it's squished

Pift pift the sifter's swift

Drip drip

milk into the batter bowl slips

MOO-MOO MILK

Mash

mash

I love to smash

Twinkle twinkle goes the salt I sprinkle

Sizzle sizzle the butter frizzles

Whoosh whoosh goes the sugar I push

Plop plop eggs into the batter glop

Twisk twisk goes Pop Pop's whisk

Whrrr whrrr
the bender blender purrs

Pound pound
the batter goes round

Clack clack

goes the spoon I whack

Slurp slurp, I chirp a burp

Scrape scrape the dough, no escape

Pour pour that's what batter's for

Blat
blat

goes the batter I splat

Swipe swipe

the counter I wipe

Creak creak the oven door squeaks
Make make the hissing cake bakes

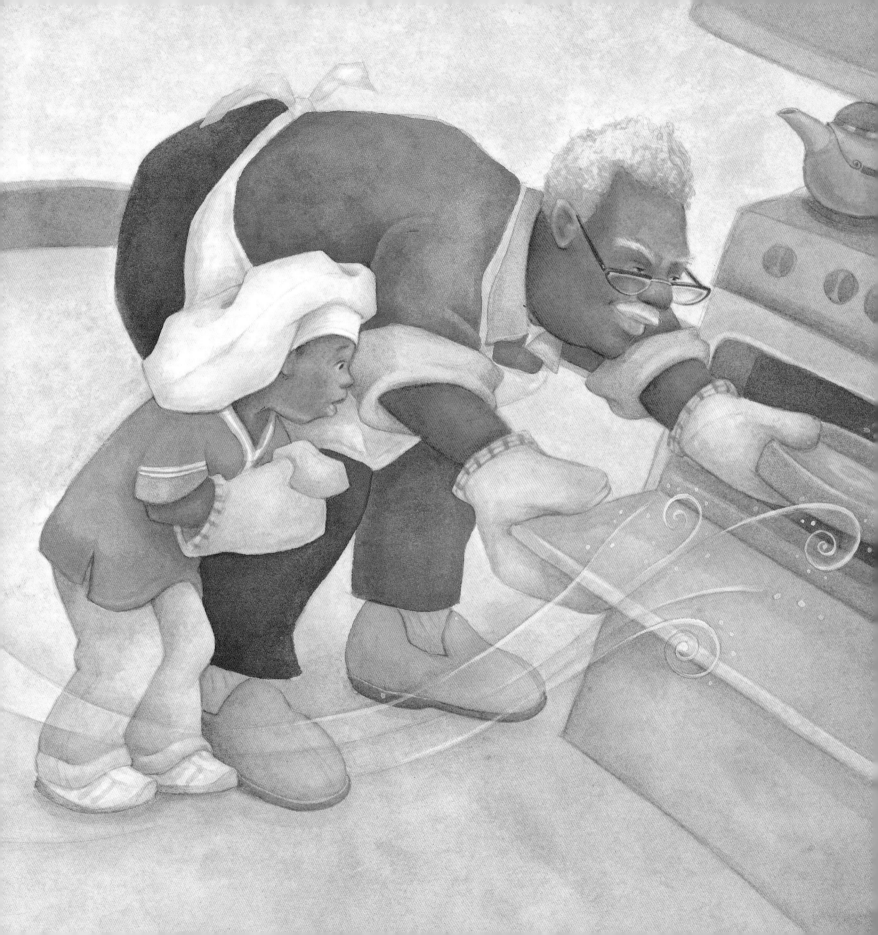

Clink

clink

dishes in the sink

Slosh

slosh

the dishes we wash

Wheet wheet

the kettle tweets

Ding ding the timer pings

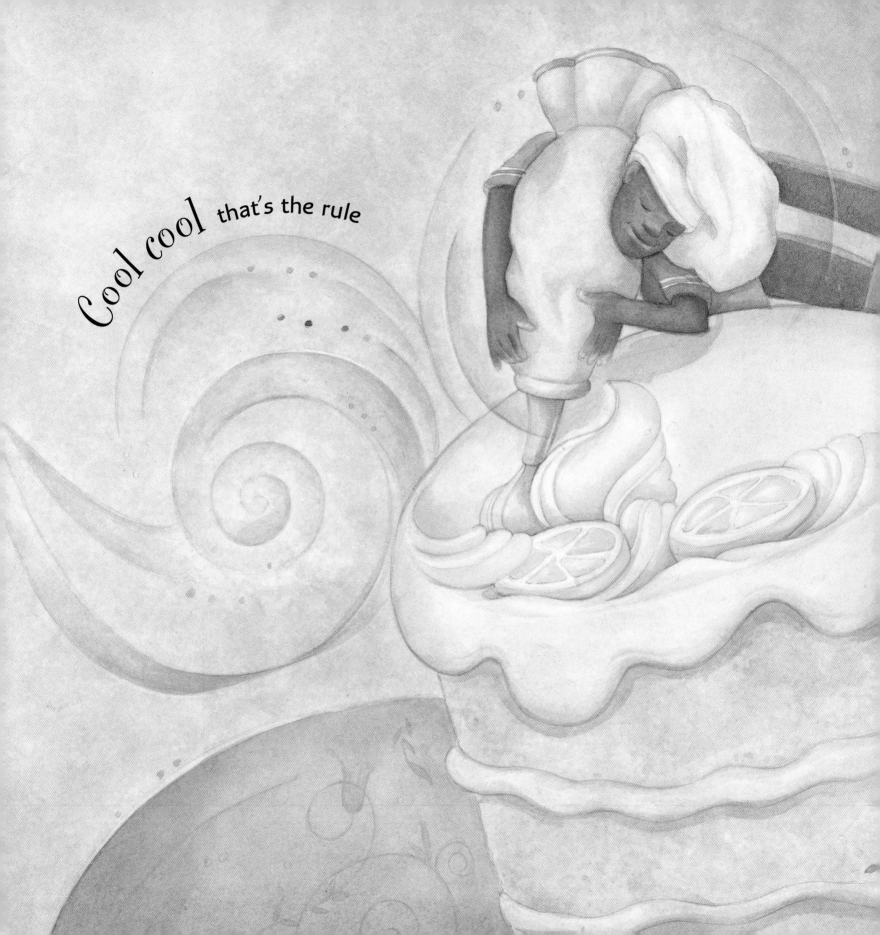

Cool cool that's the rule

Slice slice a big slice so nice

Yummy Yummy lemon cake for the tummy

I bop bop hop hop

For my top top top Pop Pop

Lemon Bar Cake Bake

Utensils Needed:

2 small bowls

1 large bowl

1 cake pan

Electric mixer (or mix by hand 350 strokes)

Large spoon

Measuring spoons

Measuring cup

Cake tester—You can use a clean toothpick

Wire rack or surface for cooling

Flour sifter (optional)

Apron

Oven mitts

Wire whisk—You can use a large fork

Preheated 350-degree oven

2-3 teaspoons cooking oil and flour (to grease and flour pan)

Ingredients:

4 tablespoons lemon oil (or lemon extract)

2 tablespoons vanilla extract

2 cups cake flour

2 teaspoons baking powder

1/8 teaspoon salt

1 cup milk

1/2 cup lemon juice (Use fresh lemons, if possible—juice 2 large lemons or 3 small lemons and take seeds out of juice)

1 1/2 sticks very softened or melted butter

2 cups sugar

3 beaten eggs